The Cl

and his daughter

Billie Potter

ISBN:
9798839990579

DEDICATION

To Sheila without whom I could not exist.

The Clog Maker and his daughter

The Clog Maker and his daughter

This story took place a long time ago, a very long time ago, in fact a very very long time ago.

It was so long ago that no-one, not you or me or anyone can really understand what it must have been like living back then.

It was a very different way of life.

Ordinary folk, folk who were called 'peasants' had no power, no say in what they did or how they lived, they had to do as they were told, they couldn't object or argue, they just had to do whatever was commanded of them.

For instance you couldn't just decide to move from where you were and go live somewhere else or anything like that. Everyone could only do what their 'Lord and Master' allowed them to do.

So, for instance, if you did want to move from your village to another one you would have to go to your 'Lord and Master' and ask for his permission, (it was always 'his', females weren't allowed such power) and sometimes he might say "yes" and other times "no", and that was that. There was nothing you could do about it.

Now, this story took place so very long ago and in another country;

There was this clog maker who lived just at the edge of a village, just where it touched the forest.

A 'Clog Maker' is someone who makes clogs, and clogs were just about the cheapest sort of footwear you could get.

Clogs are made from wood and are carved so that your feet fit in them as best they can. The clogs are hard so it's your feet that have to fit the clog and not the other way around.

The poorest people have to have clogs because they can't afford anything better, but the trouble with clogs is that they wear out very quickly.

Anyway, this Clog Maker is very good at carving clogs, his clogs were probably the most comfortable ones you were liable to get.

He had learned his skills from his father who had also been a clog maker, and his father before him, who had also been the village clog maker.

The Clog Maker's family had lived and worked in the same home for many generations and had served the village well.

The thing that allowed clogs to be so cheap was that the clog maker, every so often, went into the forest next to his home and chopped a tree down, and the tree was free therefore the wood for the clogs was free. The Clog Maker, his father before him and his father's father before that had done this and a new tree would grow where the other tree had been chopped down.

The Clog Maker would only ever take one tree at a time, new wood was always best for making clogs as it was softer and easy to carve. If he had used wood that was old and had dried out it would make carving much more difficult and take a lot longer to do, so he only ever cut down one tree at a time.

The village where the Clog Maker lived was a small village and everybody knew everyone who lived there.
It consisted of a small number of homes spread out with patches of land for each

family to grow their vegetables and to keep a few chickens.

All of the homes were small and constructed from local materials, mostly wood, straw and mud.

The Clog Maker's home was like most of the others, very basic and consisted of just one room. It was dark inside because glass was something that only the very rich had, and even they found it very expensive. So the few openings that any peasant's house had to let in light was more often closed up with a shutter to try to keep out the cold, the wind and the rain, only being open on nice warm days.

The floor was just earth and in the middle of the floor there was a circle of stones, this was where the fire sat and served as heat, light and to cook on, the fire was open with a pot hanging over it to cook food in.

The smoke from the fire drifted up into the roof and made its way out through the thatching as best it could.

The Clog Maker's home was built using wood to make a frame, then the gaps were

filled in with woven sticks which had then been covered in a mix of mud and straw which had then been allowed to dry out.
The roof was made of straw and grasses, and that was as good as it got.
The Clog Maker's workshop stood fixed to one side of his home. This was very basic and was simply some wooden beams holding up a thatched roof. The sides were not filled in as he needed as much light as he could get so that he could see to carve his clogs.

Now the Clog Maker's daughter, Ella was a beautiful young girl, well, woman really.
She was at the age where young women often find someone they like very much and get married.

The Clog Makers daughter Ella, had for some time been getting friendly with a young lad of about her own age who lived in the village, his name was Rowan. They had fallen in love with each other and now wanted to get married and start their future together.

The Clog Maker was happy that Ella had found someone that she wanted to spend the rest of her life with and he gave her his support and blessing.

However, as with everyone from the village, the young couple needed to get permission from their 'Lord and Master'.

The 'Lord and Master' of this village was a Duke, he was the younger brother of the King, and so he was very powerful.

He was not liked very much as all the people who lived under his rule thought that he misused his power a bit too much and was not very kindly towards them.

Anyway, it was to this Duke that the Clog Maker's daughter and her fiancé had to approach to get permission to marry.

The Duke's castle was built on slightly higher ground than the village which helped to make it look a very imposing building.

The Duke didn't really need a castle, there was no chance of anyone ever invading the land or challenging him in any way, he just wanted to show off his power and wealth. The castle's surrounding walls were high with little slits from which arrows could be fired, even though that was something that would never be needed.

The gate to get in was made like a drawbridge which could be raised to completely close off the entrance to the castle grounds.

Inside this outer wall was the various buildings which were needed for the castle to function.

There was the stables for the horses and the workshops for the various tradesmen to work in.

The main house where the Duke lived was very grand and looked out onto the courtyard. It was built to impress anyone who visited and that was exactly what the Duke wanted it to do.

Now, you couldn't just go up to the Duke's castle, knock on the door and expect to go in and see him.

Back then the 'Lord and Master' had special occasions in the year when he would allow the people to come and see him, to ask him to resolve problems, disputes and all sorts of other things.

The next occasion when the Duke would hold one of these 'audiences' was to be on Saint Swithun's day. These occasions were always held on a saint's day and there were usually four or five each year.

Saint Swithun's day arrived and many of the villagers and local farmers went to the castle with their requests or complaints or questions.

Ella and her young man had been up early in order to get ready for this big day. They had made sure that they were clean and had put on their very best clothing so that they would give a good impression to the Duke. Then they gathered in the castle court yard along with all the other people to await the Duke's arrival.

In the middle of the courtyard there was a canopy, it was a bit like a tall square tent but without any sides to it. Underneath the canopy was a sort of platform, a bit like a stage, a raised area, and on that was a very fine chair, it was a very elegant chair, it looked a lot like a throne with lots of carvings and brightly painted pictures and lots of gold as well. It was very impressive, which is what the Duke wanted it to be.

Ella and Rowan waited nervously with the other local folk until it was their turn to approach the Duke.

They presented themselves to the Duke with a lot of bowing and curtseying, making sure that they made a good impression. They addressed him as "My Lord" and showed all the courtesies they could think of.

They finally stood before the Duke and once he signalled that they could speak, they explained that they had been courting for some time and that they were very much in love and they were there to ask his permission to marry.

The Duke looked at the two of them for some time, he looked at the both of them from head to foot and back again, he seemed to be in deep thought.

"NO"!

That was the Duke's answer, well it was more a proclamation, more of a dictate than an answer.

Everyone had known what the young couple had come to ask, and now everyone knew what the Duke had answered.

This had never happened before, not for as long as anyone could recall, and no one knew of it ever happening in the many years before this time. It had always just been a formality, never had any 'Lord and Master' answered "no".

The young couple were shocked and completely baffled, and they along with everyone else there had no idea why this had happened, but it had and the Duke's answer was absolute, they could do nothing about it. They could not marry.

Ella had no idea why they had been refused consent, but they must have done something wrong to make the Duke act the way he had. Before Ella and Rowan left the castle the Duke commanded that she return with her father the Clog Maker.

The young couple had rushed back to her father's hovel and told him what had happened, and then they all rushed back to the castle to see what the Duke wanted with Ella's father.

It wasn't long before Ella, her father and Rowan returned and stood in front of the Duke.

The Duke beckoned the Clog Maker to approach him and once the two men were close together the Duke said;

"I want your daughter as MY wife".

This obviously was why the Duke had refused her permission to marry Rowan. He, the Duke had looked at her and desired her and decided that she should be his.

The Clog Maker was somewhat taken aback by this 'request' and looked startled.

The Duke repeated to him what he wanted, that Ella should be his.

The Clog Maker backed away from the Duke to rejoin his daughter Ella and told her what the Duke had said.

There was a discussion between them before the Clog Maker returned to the Duke.

"My daughter says that she is in love with Rowan and will only marry him" said the clog maker.

The Duke said in a very determined and threatening voice;

"She will NOT marry that man, she WILL marry me, DO YOU UNDERSTAND".

The Clog Maker once again returned to his daughter to give her the Dukes message.

Ella looked at the Duke with horror.

She was young, only just becoming a woman, and he was old, very old. He was also not at all a desirable prospect, he smelled and his teeth were awful, they had long since been white and where they were not yellow they were brown, where they were not brown they were black and where they were not black they had rotted away completely. He was fat and dirty and there were stains all down the front of his clothes were he dribbled and spilt his food and drink. No he was not desirable at all.

Again Ella and her father talked about the Duke's 'proposal' but between tears and sobs Ella made her feelings very clear to her father.

So once again the Clog Maker climbed up the steps to the Duke to inform him that Ella didn't wish to marry him.

The Duke became furious and shouted at the Clog Maker, obviously expecting him to command his daughter Ella to obey.

The Clog Maker loved his daughter too much to force her into a marriage against her will and explained to the Duke that no one could force another person to marry against their will, it was the law and no marriage could take place without the consent of both people.

The Duke was now very angry and he shouted at Ella that she would come crawling on her knees begging to marry before he had finished dealing with her, Rowan and her father.

Before the three of them could leave the castle grounds a couple of the Duke's guards stopped Rowan and told him that he could not leave and was now a servant to the Duke, effectively making him a prisoner in the castle and making it impossible for the young couple to meet again.

It was a few days later that one of the Duke's household servants called at the Clog Makers home.

This servant had been sent to enquire if Ella had changed her mind yet.

She had not.

The Duke's servant then informed the Clog Maker that the Duke, his Lord and Master had decided that the Clog Maker could no longer cut down and use trees from the woods to make his clogs and would not be allowed to do so unless and until Ella changed her mind and agreed to do as the Duke wished.

The Clog Maker didn't just make clogs for the local village folk there were other villages and homesteads near by and some a little further away who's families relied upon this clog maker for their clogs. So the little stock of wood that he had would soon run out and he would not be able to make any more clogs, and in turn he would not be able to make a living to keep himself and his daughter with food or even a home.

It was a short time after this that one of the village hovels needed some repair work.

None of the homes were particularly well built and so keeping them repaired was a frequent event.

This particular home needed one of its timber joists renewing, that was a large piece of wood in the framework which helped hold the building up.

It was normal for the villagers to help each other out on these occasions, so a few of them went off into the woods to select a tree to make the replacement timber from.

Of course the Clog Maker was very much involved with this activity as he had all the tools necessary for cutting down trees and working with the wood.

After a lot of hard work, after the tree had been selected and cut down, then cut to size and placed where the old beam had been everyone celebrated as they always did.

It was while the villagers were toasting the new bit of the building that someone suggested that the old beam might be useful to the Clog Maker, as everyone knew what had happened and that the Duke had forbidden him to cut down any new tree to make clogs from. He wasn't the only villager to suffer at the hand of the Duke, many of them had been forced to swap their good bits of land for his bad bits or to pay higher 'taxes' or undertake more unpaid work for him.

The Duke couldn't object to the Clog Maker using old timbers and it was the law that villagers could cut down trees for the repair of their homes. So that is what happened, and it wasn't very long before a few other villagers 'decided' that their houses needed repairing too, providing the Clog Maker with even more wood.

The Clog Maker would have much preferred newly cut trees as the wood was much softer and easier to carve, however as he wasn't allowed to do this anymore the old timber would at least allow him to continue making clogs.

Because the old wood was so much harder than new wood it took the Clog Maker a much longer time to carve the clogs and it was much harder work for him.
However, he was a very determined man and still wanted to make the best clogs that he could, he therefore set about carving clogs from this new source, the old house timbers.

He worked very hard and although it was taking him much longer to carve the clogs, these new ones made from old wood were turning out to be much better and longer lasting than his previous clogs.

Days, weeks, months went by and the reputation of the Clog Maker's harder wearing clogs, these harder ones, spread further than just his usual clients.
After a while, occasionally someone would come from much further away to ask him to make them a pair of these clogs.

It was not a big surprise when one day a young man with a very different accent arrived at the Clog Maker's workshop to enquire about his clogs.

He introduced himself as 'Castellan' and said that he travelled around the country a lot and had heard about the clogs which came from this Clog Maker and so he decided to visit the village to see for himself.

The Clog Maker was always happy to get new business as it made life a little easier with every extra sale he made.

This new client seemed to be very interested in the Clog Maker's clogs and asked a lot of questions about them and also about the Clog Maker, why he had started making clogs from old hard wood as well as questions about life in this particular village. The Clog Maker was very careful about what he said because he didn't want any bad reports reaching his 'Lord and Master', the Duke, and he didn't know this new client at all.

However Castellan was very engaging and seemed to already know much of the story behind the Clog Maker's situation.

After a while Castellan asked the Clog Maker to carve him a pair of clogs, he said that he wanted them for a very special occasion and so requested that the Clog Maker carved some pretty figures on the outside of the clogs.

The Clog Maker was famous locally for doing this, often for special occasions like weddings and special festivals. He was skilled at carving and could carve all kinds of designs such as animals and flowers, well almost any design which his customer asked for.

Castellan asked for flowers and leaves and especially two hearts intertwined in each other, also a pair of doves on each clog plus anything else which the Clog Maker thought would look good.

It was getting late in the afternoon by the time the two men had agreed on the design of Castellan's clogs and the Clog Maker said that it would be the following day before he could have the clogs ready.

Castellan seemed content with that and asked if there was anywhere in the village where he could stay for a night or two.

The Clog Maker was a little surprised by this as Castellan was obviously a 'free man', he seemed to be well educated and of 'good birth'. The Clog Maker said this to him explaining that there wasn't really anything which would be suitable in the village for such a man as Castellan but suggested that the Duke in his castle would undoubtably give him hospitality and shelter as he enjoyed showing his castle to his 'well bred' visitors.

Castellan didn't seem at all enthusiastic at this suggestion and told the Clog Maker that he always tried to avoid such encounters and that he much preferred to mix with 'ordinary' folk.

Castellan also explained that he travelled around the country listening to and collecting stories such as myths and local legends and also collecting folk songs, which he would then write down. This was how he earned his living, he was an itinerant story teller moving from one place to another, so he much preferred to stay with village folk where he might hear new stories.

Eventually, after a long discussion between the two men Castellan persuaded the Clog Maker to let him stay at his hovel.

The Clog Maker had explained that it was just one room in which everything happened, cooking, eating and sleeping and that there was no privacy, but this didn't deter Castellan, not one bit, and so it was agreed that he would stay the night, perhaps even two nights.

After the Clog Maker had finished his work for the day the three of them, Castellan, the Clog Maker and his daughter Ella sat near to the fire in the centre of the home.
Ella had taken care of the meal as she always did, which was a sort of watery stew continuously cooked in a pot hung over the fire and into which things were often added. There was the occasional bit of meat but mostly it was vegetables and grains which

slowly softened and became edible as they slowly warmed over the hours and days.

The meal was simple but Ella managed to make it tasty by adding different herbs, spices and an occasional piece of animal fat.

It was all that they could afford, as it was for all of the villagers.

Castellan sat and ate the meal and said that it was very good and that he appreciated Ella's cooking skills.

After the meal was over Ella kissed her father on the top of his head and then left the home, leaving Castellan and her father talking.

The two men sat near the fire drinking honey mead, which is a bit like beer, and they talked.

They swapped stories about giants and fairies and all sorts of tales that they had heard and the time passed as the two men drank the honey mead and chatted. The Clog Maker felt more and more relaxed with Castellan and began to open up a little bit more about his life and about the village 'goings on'.

At one point the conversation drifted, with a little help from Castellan, to the business of clog making, and about how the Clog Maker had learned his trade from his father and that had been the way for a number of generations.

The Clog Maker seemed a little bit sad when he talked about this and Castellan asked him why this was so.

The Clog Maker explained that he would have no one to pass his trade on to.

Castellan said that his daughter, Ella was a very attractive young woman and was bound

to marry and have children, but the Clog
Maker explained that she would not marry.
After more questions from Castellan the
Clog Maker confided that Ella was already
in love with Rowan, a local young man, but
the Duke had forbade their marriage because
he wanted to Ella for himself, against her
will.

The Clog Maker said that Ella would much
prefer to remain unmarried rather than to
marry the Duke, who was very old and
undesirable.

Castellan nodded, he seemed to both
understand and somehow already knew the
story.

The Clog Maker also told Castellan that the
reason Ella had gone out, as she did every
evening, was to stand outside the castle
walls and sing, sing so that Rowan could
hear her, and often when he could, he would

sing back to her. This was their only way of communicating and letting each other know that they continued to be in love.

The next morning the Clog Maker began working on Castellan's clogs.

First he had to choose very carefully the piece of wood from which to carve the clogs.

He told Castellan that it would take some time to carve the clogs because the wood was hard and because Castellan wanted all the extra carved designs on the clogs.

Castellan spent his time between watching the Clog Maker carving and walking around the village and the local fields talking to the other villagers as they went about their work.

Castellan was very good at chatting with the ordinary folk and seemed to be able to get them to relax and tell him all sorts of things that were going on locally.

A good part of the day had passed before the Clog Maker had completed Castellan's clogs, but they were beautiful when he had finished them, and Castellan seemed to be very pleased with them saying that they were exactly what he wanted.

Because it was late in the afternoon Castellan persuaded the Clog Maker to let him stay another night.

The Clog Maker was happy for this anyway because he had enjoyed the previous evening sitting by the fire, drinking honey mead and talking.

This evening was much the same as the previous one with the three of them having a meal together, Ella leaving to stand by the castle walls and sing to Rowan and the two men left sitting by the fire, drinking honey mead and talking, telling yarns to each other.

The next morning Castellan left the Clog Maker and the village.

Before he left he told the Clog Maker that his visit had been both enjoyable and a great value to him, he also said that he hoped that they would meet again sometime.

He then said his goodbyes to the Clog Maker and to Ella and disappeared back into the countryside from where he came.

It was a month or so later that all the excitement began. Well, it was exciting for the Duke, for everyone else in the castle and beyond it was a lot of running around getting things ready, cleaning, tidying, repairing and so on, a lot of hard work.

The Duke was to receive a visit.

He had received the notification of the visit and this was going to be a very important visit.

The Duke's nephew Prince Gawain was coming to the Duke's castle on an 'Official' visit.

Prince Gawain was the son of the King and the King was the Duke's older brother.

Many years ago the two brothers had 'fallen out' over something that the Duke had done and that was why he lived so very far away from the Royal Palaces.

This visit by his nephew the Prince must mean that he has been forgiven and that he would now be welcome back into the family, and that would make him even more important than ever.

So, everything must be right for this Royal visit. The castle must look resplendent, the village must be clean and tidy and the villagers must all be there to welcome this Prince and show how happy they are, and how much they love the Duke, their 'Lord and Master'.

The day arrived on which this Prince was due to visit the Duke.

All the peasants in the village were washed and had put clean smocks or tabards over their tatty, shabby, patched and worn out clothes so that they all looked tidy, hiding the reality of their lives from the Prince and his retinue.

They all stood around waiting for the Prince to arrive, all under orders from the Duke to look happy.

The sound of the drum beating out a marching rhythm signalled the approach of the Prince's group.

At the front of the group were the Prince's soldiers and then his guards, many of them carrying banners and flags bearing his Coat of Arms, all marching ahead of his horsemen who were also his guards and soldiers. Then his personal guards on horseback, both in front and behind him, ensuring his protection.

Of course as the Prince passed by all the villagers, the peasants bowed their heads and looked at the ground. It was forbidden for anyone other than his fellow prince's,

Dukes, Barrons and the like to look directly at him unless given permission by him.

After he had passed and gone to the castle there was a whole lot more in his group following on.

There were more foot soldiers and then there were carts and wagons full of equipment pulled by big horses and they were followed by all the people that were needed to keep the Prince in his lifestyle. So there were cooks and butchers and various others who dealt with feeding him and the rest of his band.

There were people who looked after all the horses and others who could fix and repair anything that got broken, and servants who looked after his clothes and other personal things, in fact there seemed to be a endless stream of people all dedicated to looking after him. He was indeed a very important

Prince, and one day he would be the King, and it seemed that he intended to stay at the Duke's castle for more than just a few days.

Over the next several days there was much activity in the castle. There was a lot of comings and goings to and from it with messengers and soldiers and Aids to the Prince and various carriages going in and out, many venturing far beyond the village, and some not returning.

There was indeed a lot of activity and a lot going on.

The villagers, including the Clog Maker and his daughter Ella kept their heads down and continued working in the fields or whatever other jobs they had to do, each trying to keep living and growing or harvesting food and earning enough to survive.

Everything went a bit quiet at the castle, none of the servants or guards or anyone came out, and no one seemed to arrive and go in, it was all very quiet for a number of days, and none of the villagers knew what was going on.

Then the proclamation came.
One of the Prince's officials stood in the middle of the village and commanded that everyone must attend the castle ground that afternoon.
Nothing more was said, no explanation, no information, nothing, so none of the villagers knew why they had been summoned.
Of course there was a lot of talk, a lot of ideas, most of which would mean even

harder times ahead for the villagers, it always seemed to be that way when they had been summoned in the past, it was never a good thing.

So that afternoon all of the villagers and the folk who lived nearby the village, and most of the locals who worked in the castle were all gathered in the courtyard of the castle.

The canopy and the raised platform were there as well as the Dukes 'throne'. That was where the Duke liked to talk at them from.

This time however it was not the Duke who came out to address them.

The first announcement was; "Bow before your Prince".

That meant that it was going to be Prince Gawain who was going to address them and they had to bow their heads and look to the ground.

"Thank you all for attending". Yes, that is what the Prince said, "Thank you all for attending".

None of the villagers was sure what to make of that, the Duke had never started one of his 'talks' like that.

Was the Prince 'softening them up' for some harsh news?

Murmurs went around and the villagers nervously rocked from one foot to the other, no one was sure what might happen next.

"The Duke has decided to retire from his castle and the area and to travel abroad. In fact he left to do this a few days ago, and will never return here".

This announcement made the villagers even more nervous as they couldn't imagine what would happen next, and couldn't think that it would be good.

"From now on and until my father the King or I, his heir, appoint another, I will be your 'Lord and Master'. I will make the decisions for this village and this area.".

There was still a lot of shuffling from one foot to the other amongst the villagers, everyone was nervous. Well, almost everyone.

The Clog Maker's mind had been triggered and he couldn't help feeling that the voice of the Prince was somehow familiar. He was trying to think where he had heard that voice or a similar one before, then it came to him. He had momentarily stopped listening to the Prince as his mind tumbled.

It was very similar to Castellan's voice. That was it, it was very similar.

But Castellan was an itinerant story teller, so perhaps he came from a similar part of the country to the Prince. Yes that must be it.

Whilst the Clog Maker had been thinking he had missed what the Prince had been saying. The Prince had called the villagers one by one and by name and restored to them the strips of land which the Duke had taken from them, or told them that they didn't have to pay the extra taxes which the Duke had imposed on them and various other things which the Duke had done.

This Prince seemed to know a lot about what had been happening in the village and he seemed to be putting right what everyone thought was wrong.

Suddenly the Clog Maker heard his name being called out by the Prince and so he moved forward to stand in front of Prince Gawain.

"You may look up to me" said the Prince and the Clog maker nervously looked into the Princes face.

The Prince had a bit of a grin on his face and his eye winked at the Clog Maker.

The Clog Maker couldn't quit believe what was happening, it was Castellan, he and Prince Gawain were one and the same person.

"You may cut down trees to make your clogs", the Prince said with a smile, "and I hope you make many more clogs in your life". There was a certain softness and affection in the Prince's voice.

He then said; "I believe you have a daughter, Ella".

The Clog Maker could hardly speak so he nodded.

Ella came and stood next to her father and held his hand tightly.

The Prince looked down to Ella and asked; "Are you still in love with Rowan, and would you marry him if you could"?

Ella could hardly contain herself and blurted out; "Yes, …..yes My Lord, …. Yes"!

At that moment the Prince waved at Rowan
who had been standing nearby for him to
stand next to Ella, which he did.

"Do you Rowan still wish to marry Ella"?

"Yes my Lord, I really do" was his reply.

The Prince suddenly, as if from nowhere,
produced a pair of clogs and said to Rowan;

"Then you had better have these clogs to get married in".

They were the very same clogs which the Clog maker had made for Castellan, the ones with the two doves and the two hearts carved in them.

A year later the village was a much happier place for all of the villagers to live in, the Clog maker was very contented making clogs and his daughter Ella and Rowan were now proud parents to a baby boy who would one day learn the clog making trade and take over from his grandfather, and become the village Clog Maker.

Billie Potter 2022

**_Other children books by Billie Potter
published by Amazon:_**

The Sophia adventures

Freya's fantasy stories

The lost Goddess

James and the ancient woodland
creatures

Tansen's snowy playground & Angels of
the mountain

One summer with Rosie

Jessica's village

Megan's adventures in the big little
world

Short stories for small people

Ash

The meeting room

Ninja worms

Printed in Great Britain
by Amazon

82914558R00037